The Little Angel Books Series

Animal Tales

Spiritual Lessons from Our Animal Friends

Written & Illustrated
by Leia A. Stinnett

Cover art by Leia Stinnett

ISBN 0-929385-96-9

Published by

StarChild Press
a division of
Light Technology Publishing
P.O. Box 1526
Sedona, Arizona 86339
(520) 282-6523

Printed by

MISSION POSSIBLE
Commercial
Printing

P.O. Box 1495
Sedona, AZ 86339

CONTENTS

NAILS

Animals are very special friends. They are loyal no matter how we treat them. They bring us joy. They teach us about unconditional love.

Every part of God's creation works together in harmony, learning from and teaching each other. If we pay attention we can learn some very important spiritual lessons from our animal friends, whether they are our pets or animals that live in the forest, the mountains or desert.

Animal Tales brings to you many wonderful animals with spiritual insight. Pay close attention to the messages of these special animal "angels" as they help you better understand that part of you that is God.

Meet Arnold Ant . . .

Have you ever seen or owned an ant farm, a small plastic box that is clear on one side, allowing you the joyful experience of watching an ant community come into being? If you have, you were probably amazed at how quickly the ant community planned and developed a whole section of tunnels in which to live, store their food and care for their young.

Meet Arnold Ant, or Arnie, as he is best known in the ant community. Compared to humans Arnie is tiny, but just try to keep up with this fast-moving little guy. It isn't easy.

Arnie would like to share some very important spiritual lessons with you.

First, **be patient**. Arnie and his ant family are careful planners. They are very happy to patiently watch their dreams being built a little at a time. This is one quality many of us wish we had. The ant community carefully checks out the area where they want to build, feeling as a group whether or not the area is right for their needs, and well-protected from the rain, wind and cold or any creatures who might find them to be a tasty meal.

Arnie and the ant community carefully plan and work a little at a time to create the perfect space where they will be happy. "Plan carefully," Arnie reminds us. "Focus on what you want to do. Give your project a lot of positive energy. Be patient until your plan becomes a reality. It is important to move slowly so you do not have to do part of your project over."

Not all of us are patient. We hurry through homework assignments so we can go outside and play with our friends or watch a favorite television program. What often happens, however, is that our homework takes even longer to complete because our mind is not on our homework but on what we would rather be doing. We make more mistakes when we don't focus on what we are doing in the moment. We end up being very frustrated with the whole situation.

When we are patient we complete our assignments on time and more accurately. We keep a positive attitude. Then we have lots of time to play with our friends and do the things we enjoy most.

Second, **living in a community**. Can you imagine what it would be like to live in a place where everyone shared equally in the work as well as in the fun? Wouldn't the world be a much happier place if everyone had all they needed — plenty of food, clothing, a nice home and so on? There are many people who are now working to create this type of living environment, which we call a "community."

Arnie, his ant family and friends live in a community. "It is very important to consider the feelings and needs of others as well as our own," Arnie says, "and to learn how to share without expecting anything in return. When we all work together we can build a community where everyone who participates lovingly and honestly will be happy and have everything they need in life."

"What are some important things you could do to help make a stronger community of sharing at home?" Arnie asks. "How might you make Mom's and Dad's jobs a little easier? Any ideas?"

Third, **listen to your inner voice**. Arnie and his friends always seem to know where to find food and shelter. Arnie never seems concerned about going without. He always knows that whatever he needs is and will be available.

"By listening to your inner voice," Arnie shares, "you can be very clear on where to find whatever you need, how to go about collecting it, making sure it is available and so on." Arnie points out the danger in an ant community, or any community for that matter, is when everyone listens to the advice of others. For example, "It's over here. No, over there. No. No. You are both wrong. It's over here."

Can you imagine millions of ants, each having a different belief, trying to talk each other into going this way or that? Can you imagine the confusion?

Arnie's lessons include:

1. Listen to your inner voice. In this way you know God is guiding you in what is right for you in the moment.
2. Create community at home. Help out at home so no one feels he or she has to do all the work.
3. Be patient.
4. Make work fun, a game. Take time to play and laugh. It is said that laughter is the best medicine and that it can cure even the most trying day.
5. Think in terms of "we" instead of "me." We must work together to make the world a better and happier place. "We" equals oneness — all one family. "Me" equals separateness — the feeling of I am alone here on Earth.

Meet Barnie Bear . . .

What would you do if you came face to face in the woods with Barnie Bear? You might be so surprised you would not be able to move. Or you might just want to run as fast as you can and hide where he couldn't find you.

Fear, however, is not what Barnie is here to teach us. He certainly does not want us to be afraid of him. He does ask us to respect his space. We all find it important to have a place to be alone and do what we want without having someone talking to us or disturbing us in some way.

Barnie does not have "bad days." He awakens every morning to the bright sunlight warming the Earth and all the beautiful trees and flowers in his woodland home. He stretches his body and raises his nose into the air to sniff the different aromas.

Aha! My favorite smell — honey! Barnie smiles a big bear smile. Bears love honey, you know, and they are very grateful to all the little honey bees who have collected the pollen from the flowers to make the sweet, sticky treat. Barney doesn't even mind a few stings on the end of his nose because he feels the reward of the sweet honey is worth every bit of the pain.

Barnie laughs, "Don't let anything stand in

your way of reaching the goal you want to achieve. Whatever you want to be in life, whatever you want to experience, simply focus your thoughts on that goal. Know you will achieve it. There is no such thing as failure unless you never try. Boy, I sure would be sorry if I didn't try for that honey. Even if the bees did sting me, it was worth it."

Of course, Barnie doesn't want us to get stung by bees or get hurt in any way. However, he shares with us that many times in our life we meet certain obstacles in our path that can be painful to us mentally, emotionally or physically. We might lose a close friend or our job. We might volunteer to do a special project for the teacher only to have that project given to our best friend.

Barnie points out, "Whenever we go after something special we want, really focusing on our intention, that goal can be reached easily unless we get in our own way with negative thoughts. We can be afraid we will not get what we want and others will make fun of us. We might feel we will never get it because we don't deserve it."

"And, I might add," continues Barnie, "if you don't get exactly what you thought you wanted, just know something better is coming your way. Many times God points us in a different direction for our own good so our goal can be reached more easily, or so we can learn some important lessons along the way."

"Take time out of your busy day to get quiet and go within yourself . . . meditate," Barnie reminds us. "Here we can listen to God." Every winter Barnie takes time out for his own special experience with God. Finding a nice, warm cave, Barnie climbs into a cozy corner for a long winter "nap." While sleeping Barnie has time to reflect on what he has learned over the past months and to ask himself, "What do I still need to learn? Where do I go from here? How can I accomplish this or that?"

Barnie teaches us to:

1. Set your goals (those things you want to accomplish in life); focus your attention and energy on them and *know* you will achieve them.
2. Begin each day with a smile on your face. When you follow this simple rule you will never have a "bad" day!
3. Respect other people's private space. Ask other people to respect your space. If you need quiet time, go where you will not be disturbed.
4. Take time out to be quiet, go inside and listen to God's message for you. When life is not going as you might like it to, go into the silence and just be. Listen!

Meet Billy Beaver . . .

In the fall Billy Beaver is very busy building a nice solid home to protect him and his family from the winter cold. Billy takes his time to make sure the foundation of his house is solid and secure. He does not want all his hard work washing downstream with the first heavy rains of the season.

Billy is very industrious. Rather than just sitting on a rock thinking and dreaming about his home, he gets in and does it. You won't find Billy waiting for someone else to come along and do it for him. He knows the importance of working on his home now, that if he waits too long he could spend winter out in the cold.

Billy follows his *intuition,* or inner guidance, in choosing the best place to build his home, a place that will offer him and his family the best protection from the winter cold.

"When you listen to your intuition," shares Billy, "you are better able to quickly find the perfect solution to any challenge that might come up in your life."

"Each of us has a foundation, or base upon which we build our life experiences," Billy adds. "We are all part of God. Our foundation is God. So if we strengthen our connection, or foundation to God and build our 'home' based on faith and love, we can live our life without fear or any other negative thoughts, feelings or emotions."

Billy's family and friends share in the building process so no one feels he or she has to do it all by him/herself. By listening to and sharing in the experience with others, Billy learns new and better ways of constructing his home.

"It is better to share our ideas with others," Billy points out, "to be open to learning from one another. Each of us has something important to teach and share."

Billy Beaver always makes more than one doorway in his home so he has more than one choice in entering or leaving the structure. He is never stuck or trapped in one place, even if rocks or sticks block one of his doorways.

"Welcome new experiences," says Billy. "Keep an open mind. Be aware that there is always more than one way of thinking, believing and doing. Be flexible, willing to make changes in your life."

As Billy and his family work on the new home, should a part of it crumble into the water, they laugh as they gather new pieces of wood to rebuild the damaged area. Adding the new pieces to the house they realize the importance of building it stronger, doing it a little differently than before or using different sizes of wood than before. Billy encourages, "Never give up simply because something didn't work out the way you expected it to. Don't get angry! Just keep on trying, believing in yourself, designing your life the way you want it to be. Remember, we do have the power to create anything we want here on Earth."

As a reminder Billy shares these important points:

1. Never give up! There is no such thing as failure unless you never try.
2. Make your dreams come true — act on them!
3. Working and sharing with others makes your job easier and much more fun!
4. Be open to new ideas. Look at all the possibilities. Decide which one feels right for you. Don't get stuck in believing one way is the only way.
5. Let your work become play. When you enjoy what you are doing, your work becomes fun; the project is completed much faster and easier. God wants us to have fun, to enjoy our life experiences in a positive way.
6. Build your life around the way you feel it should be built, rather than how others want or expect you to build it. When you build a strong foundation based on God and faith, and use your intuition and your God-given gifts, you will be able to easily and lovingly move through any challenge life might place in your way.

Meet Ben Buffalo . . .

Many years ago in the western Plains of the United States herds of wild buffalo roamed, grazing on the lush grasses that were plentiful in the area. To the Plains natives the buffalo meant life. He was their source of meat. His hide was made into warm clothing for protection from the winter cold and also used to make warm blankets and to cover the wigwams. His hooves were melted down and made into glue.

Every part of the buffalo was used — nothing was wasted. The Native Americans knew that as long as the buffalo was present in their neighborhood, they would have all they needed to survive in the harsh land. They respected the buffalo, taking only what they needed. The buffalo and the Plains people lived in harmony and balance.

Ben Buffalo might seem a bit strange in appearance. He appears a bit front-heavy, with lots of thick, long shaggy hair draped over his shoulders and front legs. He looks a little frightening as he quietly grazes, yet there is an energy about Ben that says he is very loving and gentle.

It is said that Ben came to give of himself fully and completely so that humankind could survive and prosper. This gift of life, this total sense of sacrifice on Ben's part, is shown through the help Ben has given to the Plains natives, who could not have survived without his presence and unconditional love.

To give unselfishly as Ben has done requires us to unconditionally love all creation. This means we do not judge, criticize or harm in any way another plant, animal, rock or human being. Many of us have some difficulty with this lesson because it is too easy to jump to conclusions about another person, to ridicule someone to feel better about ourselves and so on. To give as Ben has given we must share with others unconditionally, without expectations that they will give back.

"Examine all the wonderful things you have been given on Earth," says Ben proudly. "Appreciate each of them equally no matter what their size — large or small. How many times do you expect someone to give you something or do something for you that you want them to do? Do you say thank you, even for the little things people do for you? Are you grateful for the good food you have, the clothes you wear, your family and friends, your good health? Be thankful for each wonderful gift. Appreciate all things equally. Appreciate life as a gift in itself."

Ben is very much at peace within himself. He projects this sense of peace outwardly as he grazes. He does not let whatever is going on around him disturb his quiet time. He does what he has to do to take care of himself and his family. He does not get caught up in what is happening in the world unless it affects him personally.

Ben chooses a simple life of peace and serenity. These are the qualities most important to him. He makes sure people know that these are the qualities needed to live a happy life, that living simply is important to one's spiritual progress.

"Here are my simple rules to live by," Ben offers:

1. Take only what you need. Be grateful for all that you have. Share with others unconditionally. Love all creation equally.
2. Always do your best. Be happy. Help other people without expecting anything from them in return.
3. Respect all life; respect others. Love all of nature and treat all living things as you would like to be treated.
4. The universe is abundant. Remember, what you give out from your heart will always come back to you in many ways greater than what you gave.

Meet Bonnie Butterfly . . .

Everything in our universe operates on the basis of cycles and change: Day turns to night; fall becomes winter; winter becomes spring; spring becomes summer; summer turns to fall. These are cycles and they occur without anyone taking an action to create them. They are part of God's design of perfection in our world and each cycle plays an important role in our life.

Bonnie Butterfly is an excellent teacher when it comes to explaining cycles. Bonnie's life begins as a tiny egg. She leaves the comfort of the egg to become a caterpillar, eating and storing food in her body for her long nap. The caterpillar then sheds her skin and begins the quiet stage of her life, in which she is called a *pupa*. She prepares for the next cycle of her life by weaving around herself a comfortable cocoon, which protects her from the weather and other creatures. The cocoon Bonnie weaves is a reminder for each of us to wrap ourselves in God's protective cocoon of white light.

At the perfect time, Bonnie begins to emerge from the cocoon. Her wings are wet and shriveled. The warm Sun soon dries her beautiful wings, which reflect a rainbow of colors. Bonnie tries out her wings and her newfound freedom, flitting softly among the flowers of the garden. The sunlight is warm and comforting. Bonnie is happy to be alive.

"You know," Bonnie shares, "we can see how cycles affect us in our daily life. For example, in relationship to creation, the egg represents the forming of ideas in our mind — things we want to develop.

"In the caterpillar and pupa stages we create our ideas in the physical world. We start putting the pieces together. We write down our ideas and what will be needed — people to help us, materials to use in the project, time needed to complete the project and so on.

"As we enter the cocoon stage, we check the idea out with our *inner knowing*. We go within ourselves and review our idea, asking, 'Are we going about the project in the right way? Do we need to change anything before we create it?' We wait. We listen. We know.

"Finally the idea is created. It is time to share our joy and the project with others."

Bonnie continues, "We can also see spiritual cycles of growth within ourselves. We begin with one way of being, one sense of direction. Perhaps we do not relate to the world in a spiritual way. Then we begin to change.

"We look at what we have been doing and ask, 'What needs to change here?' We begin to have experiences we do not feel comfortable sharing with others. We make this connection to our inner voice and begin to rely more on God's recommendations than those of other people, or our own conscious thoughts.

"From this place of silence we emerge with a different way of seeing things in the world. We feel lighter, more open and sensitive to the needs and desires of others. New ideas come to us. We seem to have a greater wisdom in dealing with life's challenges. This process is called *transformation*, or change.

"We must each remember that change is a positive and natural part of life. We come to Earth to learn and grow. We exist in stages and take steps. We might start in a place where we don't believe in God, or have no spiritual connection and reach a point where we feel and know we are one with God. Our lessons help us achieve our goal of returning home to God."

Bonnie shares with us:

1. Allow change in your life; through change we all become more aligned with God.
2. Each step you take brings you closer to your spiritual goals, to realize you are a part of God. Each step offers specific lessons you choose to learn as a soul. Some lessons include: patience, unconditional love, truth, separation, oneness and so on.
3. The world has been created for us to experience material things while staying connected to God. We are connected to God in our hearts.

Meet Charlie Coyote . . .

Charlie Coyote looks like a dog that's been out all night roaming around the neighborhood. You might describe him as "ruffled." But Charlie is not really concerned about the way he looks. He is concerned about finding dinner.

"Hey, what's important here anyway? Looks or chow? We should be able to just be ourselves," laughs Charlie. "We don't have to be what other people want us to be now, do we? And . . . I know lots of folks who get real upset when they make a mistake. Mistakes aren't bad things. Mistakes teach us more lessons, right?

"So . . . I'll tell you my secret about how I deal with mistakes. I laugh, a real belly laugh. After all, I have decided you can't change the situation that just happened and it happened for a reason. Hopefully you can see the humor in it while reflecting on the lesson and just try it again."

Charlie is a survivor. Nothing gets in his way of getting what he wants. He sees in his mind something he wants. He plans on a way to get it, then he goes after it. If it doesn't work out the way he planned it, he just tries something different.

"Hey, have you ever seen that cartoon about Wiley Coyote and the Roadrunner? You know how many times Wiley's plans to trap the Roadrunner come back to haunt him? Well, the point I'm making is that no matter how many times the Roadrunner escapes Wiley's clutches, he tries again and again, always with the intention of having the bird for dinner.

"And I wouldn't give up either if I were in Wiley's shoes. I believe we can all get what we want when we need something and believe in ourselves. We ask for what we want, hold the vision and there it is. It seems that there are times we really have to work hard to get what we want.

"Remember, it's your choice. You can work hard for what you want, or ask God to help you get what you want easily and without effort.

"Also, decide what you really need out of life. Don't spend all your time fretting about things. Get on with it. Laugh, play, have a party."

Yes, Charlie knows how to live. In an area where few people or other creatures would be happy, Charlie makes a comfortable home. There is always something to eat and a warm den in the side of a mountain to keep him warm. He doesn't need much to be happy.

Charlie advises:

1. Laugh at yourself when you make a mistake, when you fall down and look foolish, or when things don't go the way you might want them to go.
2. Let every experience be perfect. Don't label something right or wrong. If you don't like what you are doing or creating, change the program.
3. Never give up. If you keep trying, you will get what you want.
4. Believe in yourself. Love yourself enough to see everything in God's perfection.

Meet Dotty Deer . . .

Dotty Deer gently touches her soft nose to the fresh green grass of the meadow, sniffing out the tender new shoots she loves to eat. Butterflies dance among the colorful flowers scattered throughout the meadow. Dotty stops eating for a moment to let one butterfly land on her nose.

A very gentle creature, Dotty would never intentionally hurt another creature. "It is important to love all parts of creation unconditionally. This means we must love without judgment, criticism, opinion, fear or expectation. We must love others as God loves us. When we love everyone and everything equally, unconditionally, we feel good. We create positive life experiences rather than negative. Remember, like attracts like."

Dotty's soft brown eyes and large ears work as a team to help Dotty feel safe wherever she goes. "Every sound around us has a certain meaning. If we tune in," says Dotty, "we will always know if there is someone around who is not loving or kind or who might mean us harm. We know when the weather is about to change. We know when we need to walk away from a situation that does not work well for us.

"When we really listen," Dotty continues, "God guides us effortlessly and lovingly through our chosen experiences. Listening is important . . . I mean *really* listening. Most people just hear words. If you ask someone what you just said, many times he/she will not remember. Listening is *intuiting*. Be a good listener.

Dotty's warm, furry coat blends in well with her forest environment, making her almost invisible. She is light on her feet, so light you might not even hear her moving about the bushes and trees.

If danger approaches Dotty can count on her long, slender legs to get her out of a tight situation very quickly. Leaping gracefully over small trees, fences and bushes, Dotty is out of sight before you can blink an eye. "It is important to protect yourself. Never feel guilty about leaving an uncomfortable situation no matter what others might say. Be silent. Feel out every situation you create for yourself. Let your *inner guidance* direct you."

Of course in Dotty's life there is always the danger of hunters shooting her for sport. But she is not resentful. She believes in and teaches forgiveness. "I do my best to live a loving, gentle, happy lifestyle. I rely on my intuition to feel safe. Life is precious to all of us. We should respect life — our own and all parts of God's creation. Hunt for what you really need, not just to put a trophy on your wall. We are each here to teach and learn from each other. Yes, life *is* precious!"

Dotty reminds us:

1. Be gentle to yourself and other parts of creation — animals, plants, rocks and people.
2. Keep your eyes open; listen to and follow your intuition. Be a good listener!
3. Give yourself permission to move away from any situation that is not comfortable regardless of what others say to you or think about you.
4. Forgive anyone who has hurt you; forgive yourself. Ask forgiveness from those you have hurt. In this way you are free to move on in your spiritual journey.

Meet Dolly Dolphin . . .

If you were to visit the warm, tropical waters of the Hawaiian Islands, you might see Dolly Dolphin and her family dancing on the waves.

Dolly is known as a *spinner* dolphin. Her unique spinning motion is something to see. She leaps high above the waves and spins down into the depths of the sea in a spiraling pattern. "All of the universe moves in a spiral," Dolly points out. "Each planet, star, galaxy, nebula and so on moves in a spiral. When we spin we feel better. We stay healthier and happier because we are in harmony with the vibration of the entire universe."

Dolphins live in a group or community called a *pod.* The pod consists of several dolphin families, young and old alike. This community sleeps, eats and plays together. Each member is a team player, working for the benefit of the entire family.

"People of Earth have moved away from the experience of community or extended family. When we think of God we think of oneness, unity, one big family, where everyone is loved and feels to be of equal importance. When we separate we feel alone, out of balance," Dolly notes.

"There is a concern at this time on Earth to establish community. People realize what they have created in their experience with separation. They are now developing new places where many families come together to work, to teach their children how to survive in the world and how to live simply, sharing in community, with nature, equally. In community one person does not have to do all the work. No one goes hungry or has no place to live. Everyone shares equally in the wealth of the community. Community creates oneness."

Dolly also shares with us how important it is to breathe, that many of us breathe very shallow breaths, taking in very little oxygen for our bodies to use. "Don't just breathe because you have to," Dolly says adamantly. "Breathe deeply, as though you were inflating a balloon. Hold your breath a few moments, then blow your breath out quickly."

Dolly continues, "Your breath is life. It brings new energy to each cell of your body, to your organs, bones, muscles and skin. Your breath can help you relax in the most stressful situation.

"Your breath can easily assist you in going deeper inside yourself, where you can listen to God's messages for you. You can use your breath to take you deeper into the universe, imagining you are swimming freely with the angels, the heavenly bodies."

Dolly's special words of wisdom are:

1. Practice spinning to keep your body in balance and harmony with God's entire universe. When your body is in harmony you are happy, healthy, whole.
2. Develop a sense of community. Make friends and family important. Work together as a group rather than individually. Plan together. Accept each other's ideas. Things get accomplished much faster and easier in this way.
3. Know God loves and supports you in everything you choose to do. See and feel yourself as one with God and the universal family.
4. Breathe deeply. The breath is life; it is energy that makes your body healthy and whole. Use the breath to heal, to relax, to strengthen your connection to God.

Meet Esther Eagle . . .

In Native American teachings the Eagle is considered a symbol of the *Great Spirit*, or God. The Eagle reminds us to stay connected to God, to keep moving ahead on our spiritual path, upward, never looking back wishing one thing or another in our experiences could have been different.

High above the valley floor on a rugged mountain peak, inaccessible to other creatures or humans, Esther Eagle has built her nest. She feels safe and protected here. In fact Esther spends all of her time in very high places.

Soaring high in the sky, Esther's majestic wings keep her stable in the swiftly moving currents of the wind. She has no fear as she soars high above the valley floor and feels very much a part of the whole, of God.

Her vision is so keen that even from a great height she can spot a meal under a bush far below. If it looks like something good to eat, down she swoops, quickly grasping the unsuspecting critter in her sharp talons without ever touching the ground. And . . . *whoosh!* . . . up she goes, high in the sky to her mountain nest for dinner.

"Don't be afraid to go higher," Esther shares. "Of course I don't mean that you should put yourself in danger. What I am talking about is making changes — spiritual growth, you know.

"Sometimes as we grow spiritually, we have certain experiences other people do not have, or experiences others don't talk about. They might make fun of us, call us names and make us feel something is wrong with us.

"It takes great courage to be who we are, to allow God to guide us each day, to surrender to God — meaning we trust God will provide for us everything we need. Why, even my food comes from God. God points me in the direction of a meal through my intuition. What a wonderful gift!" says Esther proudly.

"Never be afraid," continues Esther. "Fear just gets in the way of any success you want to achieve. Fear is the opposite of love. Fear is the most negative feeling on Earth and can stop you in your tracks. Can you imagine what it would be like for me if I was afraid of heights?" Esther begins to laugh.

"Fear is an absence of light, of God. When we fill ourselves with God's love and light, there can be no fear. When we face our fears we better understand the lessons we are choosing to learn from them. We can love our fears and thereby free ourselves from the control fear has over us."

"Never look back and say, 'I wish I could have done this differently,' or 'If I had done this that way, this situation would not have happened.' You don't know that.

"With every choice you make, you learn an

important lesson of your choice. Every time you try something in a different way, you have a different experience — positive and negative. You can't change the past, what has already happened. You can, however, learn from the experience.

"Then, keep going forward. Try something different. Forgive yourself. Forgive all the people involved with you in learning your lesson. In this way you move forward in unconditional love," Esther reminds us.

Esther's lessons include:

1. Keep your eyes open. God provides for all your needs whenever you need something. Be sure to recognize God's gifts.
2. As you begin your spiritual journey, do not look back and wish you could have changed some experiences. Move forward. The more spiritually aware you become, the greater your tests. However, God never gives you more than you can handle at any one time. Ask for help; God will offer whatever you need unconditionally.
3. Have no fear. There is nothing to fear but fear itself.
4. When you feel connected to God, you feel whole, perfect and free.

Meet Horace Horse . . .

Horace Horse is very proud of his ancestors. Millions of years ago, at the time of the dinosaurs, ancestors of the modern-day horse were the size of a small dog or cat. Through the ages the horse evolved into the size you see him as today.

People of long ago learned how to ride the horse, to use him to carry their packs and pull their wagons. Horace's ancestors offered to humankind what is called "selfless" service, or giving to others without expecting anything in return. To families of the Old West the horse was a very important member of the family and was treated accordingly.

Horace stands with his head held high, displaying his fine, flowing mane. Offer him some oats and he will greet you with a friendly whinny.

"I'm very strong," says Horace. "I can handle most any load. We all need to be strong, not only in our physical body but in our mind and spirit. Strength is not intended to be used to hurt people but to help us stand in our own power in dealing with a difficult situation. Strength in spirit means strength in God — strength without fear."

Horace adds, "How many of you follow other people's advice, even when you know in your heart it is not the right thing for you to do? Do you let others make choices for you, even those that make you unhappy?

"When you don't honor your own feelings and choices, your own individuality, you give away your personal power. You might become very angry and unhappy with yourself and others. Remember, *you* are the one who chooses which way to go — to follow others or to stand in your own power and do what you feel is right.

"Sometimes when standing up for yourself, or standing in your own power, as we say," Horace continues lovingly, "you might watch your friends walk out of your life. When this happens, look at the bright side. The old friends leave so new friends who are more like you can come into your life.

"Life is a continual flow of cycles and change. Change brings new experiences, which help us move closer to God, to what we call reality."

Horace makes very wise choices. He listens carefully to his *inner voice* and follows what he feels is right, his own path. Even when someone is riding on his back, he will stop suddenly to check out a situation. If he feels it to be necessary, he will make a change in direction, taking a different path, sometimes to the frustration of the rider, who hasn't a clue as to what Horace is doing. Horace does not intentionally disobey instructions; he simply follows his *knowing* for the well-being of everyone involved.

Horace reminds us to:

1. Be strong in body, mind and spirit. Your inner strength will get you through any difficult situation. Your spirit is the strongest part of your whole being.
2. Stand up for yourself. Follow your own path. If others make fun of you, let their words pass through one ear and out the other.
3. Own your own power. Respect and honor yourself, your choices, your truth to walk away from any situation that does not feel right to you.

Meet Hallie Hummingbird . . .

A high-pitched *whirring* sound fills the air around the flower garden in your backyard. Who or what is making that sound? To find out the truth of the matter, look carefully and quickly in the direction of the sound. Study the flowers near the sound.

You will see a very tiny bird with wings moving so fast you can barely see them. Its long, pointed beak will be buried deep inside a flower, drawing out the sweet nectar from which it makes its meal.

Hallie Hummingbird must be the fastest creature on two wings. She darts up, down, from side to side, without a pause. She can even hover in one place in the air, checking out the area below for a tasty flower or any danger she might feel.

"Look carefully at every situation," Hallie points out. "Be aware of everything around you. Be ready to change direction in the moment if something doesn't feel right, or if you realize the direction in which you are going is headed nowhere."

Hallie takes time to smell the flowers, but if you try to catch her she is gone in a flash. "How would you feel if someone put you in a cage, especially after you have enjoyed years of freedom?" Hallie asks. "You know, we were all created to have fun, to be happy doing what we enjoy doing.

"People can interfere with what we want for ourselves. They can convince us we should follow their advice. If we do, we are in a sense giving up our freedom of choice, of being who we are.

"Freedom is part of our personal power experience and our desire to make our own choices — good, bad or indifferent. Always respect the freedom of others. They in turn will respect yours. God's world will then remain in harmony. Remember, none of us are happy when we are not free to make our own choices in life."

Hallie enjoys happy places and will not venture into any setting that does not make her feel good. "When you surround yourself with beauty, joy, love, you feel those energies inside yourself. What you feel, you become. What you become, you attract into your life — just think, more beautiful, joyful, loving people and experiences. Yes."

Special words of wisdom from Hallie include:

1. Be willing to make changes in your life. If you are not happy, examine the things making you feel unhappy. List the ways you can change those experiences. Then act on what you feel can help.
2. Use your energy to be happy, to help others be happy, too. Laugh out loud. Laughter makes you feel good.
3. Take time out each day for yourself. Go for a walk. Read a good book. Sit quietly under your favorite tree, or in the garden. Talk to God; listen to what God says to you. Slow down. Spend time by yourself. You will feel more peaceful, more calm.
4. Follow your feelings, make your own choices. Only you know what is right for you.

Meet Lila Lizard . . .

In the early morning the warm desert Sun gently touches Lila's still body. Sleeping on top of a big rock, the only movement you can see in Lila's body is her shallow breathing pushing her sides in and out.

As you watch her closely, you might wonder, What kind of dreams do lizards have? Well, let's ask Lila.

"Oh, I have dreams just like anyone else's," Lila replies with a big yawn. "Dreams are like little stories, telling us what we need to pay attention to each day. Dreams help us work things out that we can't seem to understand in our daily experiences. Dreams can show us things that might take place in the future, and they show us how well we are doing on our spiritual path.

"Some dreams might be very difficult to understand. They might be trying to tell us one thing while we feel they are telling us something totally different. For example, you might see a key in your dream and think you will use it to lock a door. But the key could also mean you are about to open a new door, creating a path to a new experience.

"And there are those dreams we call

nightmares," adds Lila, drawing back her shoulders to imitate someone who is showing fear. "Nightmares help us understand things we are afraid of in the moment. Once we face our fears we can laugh at them and give them a big hug. I really appreciate these dreams because I don't want to be afraid of anything. Sometimes we don't even know what we are afraid of until our dreams show us."

Here are some important tips Lila offers to help you remember your dreams:

1. Before you go to sleep tell yourself, "I will remember my dreams tonight."
2. Keep a pencil and paper or notebook by your bed. The moment you wake from your dream, write down everything you remember about the dream.
3. If you can't write it down, tell your dream to Mom, Dad, a brother or sister, friend or teacher. He/she will help you translate the dream into something you do understand.
4. Ask yourself, "What does this dream mean to me?" Write down the first thoughts that pop into your head. Your dream will mean one thing to you and perhaps something totally different to another person having a similar dream.
5. If you don't understand what your dream means, ask the angels to repeat the dream in

a way you can better understand the message. The dream will be different, but the message will be the same, just more clear each time it is repeated until you understand. Then you will move on to a different experience, a different dream.

Meet Maya Mountain Lion . . .

High above the valley floor in a small cavern hidden by the trees and bushes of the mountain's crest lives Maya the mountain lion and her family.

Maya is big and powerful. Her coat is smooth and sleek. She stands out from other animals who live on the mountain, looking very regal and majestic.

She moves alone in the wilderness, following her own inner guidance rather than advice of others. She knows what she needs to do to feed and protect her family and does so lovingly and willingly.

Maya is gentle and kind. She makes a very loving mother to her cubs, seeing that all their needs are met each day. From the moment of their birth, Maya begins teaching them how to care for themselves, how to survive in a world that is not always loving and friendly. Maya shows them how to clean themselves, to find food and shelter. She also shares one very important spiritual lesson: *Take only from nature what you need to survive!*

Most of us are comfortable in our homes. We do not think much about surviving in the wilderness and how that might feel. Maya reminds us of how important it is for each of us to know how to survive in the world without relying on material things, to follow our own inner guidance, knowing God will always provide for us when we ask for what we need and have the faith it will come to us.

As her cubs grow, Maya teaches them to climb in high places. To do so successfully, she stresses the importance of staying in balance. Maya shares with us that balance must come from being centered within ourselves, to be aligned with God's love at all times. When we are aligned with God, when we are balanced, we feel safe, courageous. We are not afraid of change, of trying new things.

It is important to Maya that we not be afraid of anything. She chooses the highest points on the mountain in which to live, feeling very safe there. This is symbolic of our desire to move closer to God. We never want to go backward. Often as we grow spiritually, we feel like we are climbing a mountain. We might feel alone in the world because others do not believe or feel the way we do. Maya reminds us, "As you leave those friends behind who do not want to grow with you, you will find new friends coming into your life who do think and feel as you do in that moment of time."

Many people do not want to be leaders. They would rather avoid making decisions for themselves and follow other people instead.

They might be afraid of being blamed for things that go "wrong," afraid of being challenged by others. Some people feel they will be left "holding the bag" and being pushed into a place of leadership because no one else wants the job. Has this ever happened to you?

"Be a good leader," Maya encourages. "Don't be afraid of trying new things or going where others are afraid to go. Speak out; defend yourselves against any challenge in a loving way. Stand in your own power. Stand up and support what you believe is right. Be honest with yourself and others. This is the way you gain respect."

Maya adds, "A good leader must have courage to stand alone when he or she believes strongly in something. A good leader shares ideas with others, allowing them to express their ideas openly. It is better to share in group discussions than to be a dictator. Everyone's voice is important."

A good leader observes the whole situation, looking at all the possibilities, working with the entire group to find the solution that benefits everyone. A good leader is honest, maintains a peaceful meeting, balances the scales. A good leader takes full responsibility for him/herself and creates positive change with a positive attitude and expression.

Remember Maya's message:

1. Be a good leader, involving the entire group in finding a peaceful solution to the problem.
2. Help change the world to a happier, healthier, more loving place by taking responsibility for yourself, standing in your own power, following your inner guidance, keeping a positive attitude toward yourself and others and creating balance in your thoughts, words and actions.
3. Simplify your life; don't take more than you really need.
4. Be centered in God. Let go of any fear of change or of trying new things.

Meet Opie Opossum . . .

Opie is a most unusual little guy with a great big heart and a very special gift. When Opie is not feeling comfortable about a certain situation or when someone has moved into his private space, and he feels he has tried everything to change the situation, he will simply lie down and play "dead." Yep, he looks just like he suddenly made his transition into the world of *spirit*, and the show looks so real that his challenger simply moves on and leaves Opie alone.

Opie shows us that because we are loving

and gentle and wish to help others, some people see us as "pushovers" or easy targets for their anger and frustration. For example, the neighborhood bully is usually larger or "tougher" than the other children. He forcibly pushes others around to get what he wants. Many children are afraid of the bully on their block and will run away, or let the bully push them around in order to feel safe. Neither the children bullied nor the bully is very happy.

According to Opie, it is important to rely on our intuition in deciding the best way out of a tight corner. We might elect to stand our ground, pretending to be unafraid, not allowing the aggressor to bully us. Or we might choose to ignore the bully, letting his hurtful words move through one ear and out the other.

"If you refuse to show emotion when someone says hurtful things to you or tries to bully you, if you refuse to get involved in their hurtful games or strike back, in most cases the bully will tire of the game and move on. If he does not leave, follow your inner guidance. You might be guided to turn and walk away rather than run," notes Opie.

Opie continues, "Don't make up excuses to your friends for what you are feeling. For example, your friends might want you to go to the river to swim. You do not feel you should go. Never feel that you have to make up an excuse such as not feeling well, or that your

Mom wants you to help her at home. Just tell the truth: 'I don't choose to go today.'"

You do not have to defend your right to just be. Just say no. You do not owe anyone a reason for your decision. Sometimes offering an excuse will only lead to more challenges for you. Like Opie, play "dead"; that is, offer no defense. When you give the situation no energy, you will be happier.

Opie warns, "Expect the unexpected. Always be *prepared*. Use your brain; think; plan. Be clever in your decisions. You never know what each new day will bring. Be assured that if you are prepared for anything, you will be able to handle all situations lovingly and effortlessly.

Pay attention to Opie's wise counsel:

1. Trust and follow your intuition, your own inner feelings.
2. Don't be afraid to be who you are rather than who others want you to be.
3. Think carefully about any situation, then act on it according to what you feel is right. Be clear in your decision. If you feel the need to walk away from any given situation, don't be concerned about what your friends will think. Smile as you walk away. Your friends will get the picture from the expression on your face.

Meet Ollie Owl . . .

W*hooooo-Whooooo* . . . Why, it's Ollie Owl, that's who! Ollie is up in his favorite tree as night falls once more in the forest. He is well-respected for two very important jobs that he performs. First, he warns the other forest creatures of any sign of danger.

Using his *inner sight,* or intuition, and keen sense of hearing, Ollie "sees" what others cannot see. When he hears something, he pauses and patiently listens to the sounds of the night. His intuition tells him whether or not danger is approaching. His early warning signal helps all the creatures better prepare for what is coming their way.

Ollie can see in the dark. "Each of you can see in the dark as well. Here, I'll show you how," shares Ollie.

"Sit quietly in your bedroom without turning on the lights. What do you see? Now, turn on the light for a moment and carefully study your room. Make a mental note of where you 'see' your bed, lamp, desk, chest of drawers, toys and so forth. Then turn out the light. Sitting quietly on your bed or in a chair, look around your room. 'See' again where everything is. The more you practice this exercise, the easier it will be for you to see in the dark, too."

"When you 'see' in this way," notes Ollie,

"you are seeing from a feeling place. You intuitively know where things are. You feel their energy."

A second job Ollie performs is that of teacher. He offers greater wisdom to those who need help in answering perplexing questions. "We're all plugged into the same Source of information, you know," Ollie explains. "That Source is God. The only challenge we have is not being quiet enough to hear God's answer, not trusting what we hear, or not acting on the information. We like to challenge everything by thinking about it. Then our ego gets in the way of what God is telling us.

"God speaks to us through our inner voice, our intuition. What is shared is always right for us in the moment; it is our own truth. But I feel we must learn to *discern* everything. Discernment means to check something out, to make sure we feel good about it before we act on it. When we receive a message about something, sit with it. Feel it.

"For example, suppose two friends are telling you two different stories about why they didn't invite you to the movies. If you release anger or any hurtful feelings about the situation (don't take it personal), go inside yourself and ask God to show you who is being truthful, then your body will reflect who, if anyone, is telling the truth. When it is truth, it feels right all over your body. When it doesn't feel right, you feel a gnawing sensation in the pit of your stomach or an energy that seems to push you back."

So Ollie's advice is:

1. Learn to use your intuition to "see" more clearly, even in the dark. When we turn on our *inner light* we can see anything, anywhere.
2. Discern *all* situations before you get involved. "Feel" it out for your own protection.
3. Be quiet. Ask God to help with situations you can't work out or understand.
4. Honor and respect yourself; you *do* have all the answers when you go within and ask God.

Meet Patty Porcupine . . .

If you have never seen a porcupine, you can only imagine how scary it might be to meet up with an animal whose body is all covered with long, sharp quills and feet equipped with very long, sharp nails. Most likely, you would turn and run away without ever really getting to know the real Patty Porcupine.

Did you know that Patty is really very loving and friendly despite her ferocious looks and bad reputation? As long as you show no fear, she will welcome you and gently eat whatever you offer that is to her liking.

"Never judge anyone by what you see on the outside," Patty reminds us, "and never be afraid of someone who looks different from you."

It is important to feel inside, in our hearts, whether it is safe for us to get to know another person better. Many people do not take time to make friends with people who are blind, deaf, without arms or legs, or those people who must spend their lives in wheelchairs — in fact, all those people who are "different."

"Remember, just because someone is not exactly like you does not mean he or she cannot be a very special, loving friend," Patty states. "Look deeper within people. Get to know that part of them that is *just like you,* that part which is God."

Patty does not worry about or fear anything or anyone. She feels safe in her protective armor of quills and reminds each of us that we, too, have a protective armor, the light of God. When we imagine God's white light all around us like a huge white bubble of light, when we call upon God and the beautiful angels to protect us, we feel safe and secure. All our fears and worries disappear.

If you ever have an opportunity to watch Patty in the woods, you will see that she is a very loving, playful little creature. She has a wonderful imagination. As she lumbers slowly through her woodland home, sniffing everything in her path, she teaches us to be open to new experiences, to keep an open mind because we never know what great new adventures might unfold.

"Each new day is unique and special, offering a whole new adventure in fun, learning experiences and growth," says Patty, smiling. "I always learn something new and meet interesting friends. I am thankful for all the wondrous gifts God brings me — a warm bed, plenty of good food to eat and fresh water to drink, wonderful, loving friends to play with and the special adventures in my forest home."

Patty points out to us that it is very important to express our gratitude to God each day for all the wonderful things we are given here on Earth, and for the beautiful Earth herself.

Patty's reminders include:

1. Always be loving and kind to *everyone* you meet.
2. Know God loves and protects you always, that you can ask God to wrap you in white light at any time to help you feel safe.
3. Always begin each new day with a big smile, an eagerness to learn new things, an appreciation for the wonderful Earth and for all the gifts God brings to each of us.

Meet Rusty Rabbit . . .

Deep beneath the cool, damp forest floor in a snug burrow lives Rusty Rabbit. Rusty is soft and gentle. He is very, very shy. At the slightest noise Rusty runs for cover, dodging whatever he thinks is after him, or planning on having him for dinner.

You might think Rusty is a big coward the way he runs and hides from every little sound. However, Rusty is not a coward. He just doesn't have the same defenses as other animals do. Antlers and claws are not part of his anatomy.

Rusty teaches us how important it is to be and feel safe, to move away from any situation that feels uncomfortable. "Don't hang around waiting to see what happens," Rusty warns. "If it doesn't feel good, get going. Ask questions later!"

Rusty reminds us that fear is a very powerful negative emotion on this Earth. "Fear can make you freeze in your tracks," Rusty warns. "When I am afraid, I run for cover, whatever cover is the closest, or I zip down my burrow deep inside the earth. Here I can look at all the things I'm fearing.

"You can, too. Suppose you are afraid of something. You duck for cover in your room — your own private space. You pull the covers of your bed over your head and begin to think about what is making you afraid.

"Grab a notebook and pencil and start writing. Write down everything you are afraid of. Look at the list. Feel the energy of each thing you are afraid of, one at a time. Ask the angels to help you send love to the fears, to yourself. Wrap yourself in a warm blanket of God's white light. Feel safe and warm. Say good-bye to your fears. Don't think about them any longer. If you pay no attention to fears, they will not be part of your experience."

Rusty continues, "God gave us a very important law to follow, different from laws people have created. This law of attraction says that whatever you think, you create. Wherever your mind is, there you are. Like a magnet, like attracts like. Be afraid, attract more fears. Be love, attract more love. Simple, isn't it?"

So follow Rusty's advice:

1. Don't let fear control your life. Face your fears. Laugh at your fears. Love them and let them go.
2. When you feel uncomfortable, move quickly to someplace you feel safe. Don't feel guilty about making a move no matter who you are with or where you are.
3. If people make fun of you for running away from a situation (as they see it), don't feel bad. We must each take responsibility for our own safety, our own experiences.
4. Being shy does not mean you are a coward or afraid of something. Sensitive people feel everything from everybody. They might have the need to move away to avoid picking up feelings that they don't like. Shyness can reflect sensitivity. Respect that quality if you have it.

Meet Ricki Raccoon . . .

At the edge of the bubbling stream, Ricki Raccoon is busy washing her dinner. Ricki washes everything before she puts it in her mouth. Does that sound familiar?

Ricki looks something like a large cat, but has two very unique features that make her stand out from the other forest creatures. Her tail has rings of black and her face is covered by a black "mask." To see her, you might think Ricki is a bandit preparing for a holdup.

"Not me!" exclaims Ricki in a loud voice. "Not me! I have no intention of doing anything you might consider 'bad.' This mask offers an important message. It is a symbol; it reminds all of us that we each have a 'mask' we try to hide behind, thinking no one will see or know who we really are and therefore we will be safe."

Ricki continues, "Sometimes people hurt our feelings. Sometimes we don't feel very good about ourselves. We compare ourselves with others and judge ourselves to be less than they are because they can do something we can't or do something better than we can, as we perceive it.

"There are those people who tease us and make us cry. We want to run and hide. But there are times we just pretend to be who we are not, just to fit in. Have you ever done that? Tried to be someone else, to do what the others do just so they will accept you?

"And what happens when you are found out?" questions Ricki. "Even if you try to hide behind the mask, the feelings are still there. Whenever someone hurts our feelings, our emotions take over. We feel bad. We cry.

"The mask might hide our face, our tears. However, we can't hide from our feelings, can we?" Ricki says calmly.

"You see, even when you wear a mask, the real you is there, waiting to be invited out into the open. As a part of God, the real you is energy, light, divine love. Wherever you go, whatever you do, the real you is there also.

"When you are unhappy or feeling hurt, feel the real you as God's love. Let that love shine from the inside out, until all you feel is love. The unhappy, unhurtful feelings will disappear. What you feel, other people feel as well. So if you are with a group of angry, hurtful people, they will begin to feel God's love. Their attitudes will change to be more loving as well. Try it. You will see what I mean," shares Ricki.

"We are all part of God. God loves us no matter what we think, say, do or feel. Even when we feel sad and alone, God is with us, God is loving us," Ricki adds.

Ricki teaches us:

1. Take care of yourself. Appreciate who you are as one with God. All those qualities God is — light, love, peace, joy, happiness, harmony, health, perfection, abundance, truth and so on — are also part of you.
2. Don't try to hide behind a mask. Stand up for yourself, be who you are. God is on your side and will help you feel strong and safe.
3. You know who you are. Many people judge others by what they see on the outside — color of skin, clothes they wear, height, weight, disabilities and so on. The true self, the real you, is on the inside. Let people talk. Let the energy move in one ear and out the other. If you don't hold on to what other people say, their words will have no power over you. Have a happy day!

Meet Sammy Skunk . . .

Imagine that you and your friends are hiking in the woods, laughing, having a great time. Suddenly, there in the middle of your path, is a small black and white animal that resembles a large cat. As it waddles out of a bush, it spots you and your friends moving closer. The little animal turns, raises his tail toward you, digs his heels into the earth, and waits to see what your next move will be.

What do you do when you realize a skunk is in the middle of the only path through the woods, blocking your passageway and threatening to give you and your friends the most unpleasant shower of your life?

You have come "face to tail" with Sammy Skunk, who has quite a reputation, you know. If you challenge him or move into his space with any intention of teasing him or causing him harm, he will spray you with a most distasteful aroma. Sammy is playful and loving . . . until you move too close, then look out! Sammy will not threaten you physically, but he will threaten your senses with a smell you will *never* forget . . . whew!

Sammy has some very important spiritual lessons to teach us. "Respect yourself enough to stand up for yourself, no matter what. And be sure to stand your ground when you know you are right, or when someone challenges you. When you respect yourself, others will see your strength and leave you alone.

"Be proud of who you are," adds Sammy. "Demonstrate that pride in the way you carry yourself. Walk with confidence, head held high. Project strength and courage in a gentle, loving way. Go with the flow of life. Don't get caught up in other people's games."

Sammy continues, "Don't let others take advantage of you or make you do things you know are wrong, simply because you want to be part of the group. When you stand up for what you believe is right, when you put out energy that says, 'I will not be part of that crowd,' and do it in a loving way, you will draw more loving friends into your life — people more like you."

As Sammy raises his tail he demonstrates he is taking a stand, defending himself from other animals or people, that he is not afraid. He does not threaten anyone but does, in fact, let it be known, "Don't come into my space unless I invite you." Sammy shares that each of us has our own personal space where it might or might not be comfortable for others to enter. If it is not comfortable, we need to feel okay in asking them to move away.

Sammy's message also includes:

1. Be who you are. Don't be afraid to be different. Don't let other people make you feel bad about yourself. Some people like to make fun of others because they are not happy about themselves. We do not have to be part of their experience. If we don't react in a negative way as they poke fun at us, they will soon tire of the game, lose interest and move on. However, if we react with anger or tears as they tease us, they will make fun of us even more.
2. It isn't easy to ignore people who are making fun of us. However, if we think about positive experiences, how much God loves us, and ask God and the angels to surround us with a warm, loving feeling, it will be easier to let go of the negative experience. The sooner we let go, the sooner we can move on to a more joyful experience.
3. Be loving, outgoing, playful. Have fun in everything you do. The next time you see Sammy in the woods, please show him some respect. Treat him as you would like to be treated and he will respect your space by not spraying you with his special "perfume."

Meet Sally Squirrel . . .

Like a flash of light, Sally scampers up the large trunk of an old oak tree to a hole that she has made into her home. As she reaches the entrance to her house, her cheeks full of nuts, she gently slides inside to deposit the precious morsels of food, where they will be well-preserved from winter weather and other creatures who might be tempted to eat them.

Like a jack-in-the-box, out of the hole Sally pops, scurrying down the trunk to gather more nuts. She will continue to gather food until she knows she has enough to last all winter. Because every winter is different in length and severity of weather, she will not gather the same amount of food this winter that she gathered for the previous winter, or the winter before that.

With a serious look on her face Sally states, "Always plan ahead. Be prepared for everything and anything. One can never plan too carefully.

"Don't get caught without the things you need to be comfortable and safe. Plan for that rainy day. Get out your rain gear. Make sure you have all the pieces and that your raincoat is in good shape," Sally laughs at the example she has come up with.

Sally continues, "Take only what you need. The Earth has been harmed by those who have and continue to take more than they need.

Some animals and plants are now *extinct* or close to extinction, which means they have disappeared from the Earth. Not one of their species remains here to enjoy the beautiful Earth.

"Forests have been cut down, so the soil has washed away. That doesn't make us squirrels very happy. The trees are our homes. They supply our food, shelter and protection. Without them, we too might be doomed.

"Even in the human world," adds Sally, "there are people who have more than others; yet they will not share what they have. They want more and more, until there is nothing more to be had. There is no room for greed in our world. When you take only what you need, as we animals do, there will always be plenty for others. No one will be hungry or without a place to live."

Before storing new food items in her home, Sally cleans out whatever is left from the previous winter's storage. "Clean out your closets," announces Sally. "If you aren't going to use something, pass it on to someone who can use it rather than stuffing it in the back of your closet or garage. What you consider junk can be something very special and much appreciated by someone else. An old coat of yours can make someone very happy if they do not have a coat of their own. Always think of others . . . recycle!"

"And by the way," Sally giggles, "just

lighten up! Many of you humans take things so seriously. You have forgotten how to play. When you simplify your life, getting rid of things that you don't need or can't use, you will feel less burdened with responsibilities. Having things equals responsibility to care for those things.

"We are here for a short time on Earth. Stop worrying about the future. Did you know you create your future? That's right. Whatever you think about you create. Your future is yours to create. In the meantime, right here and now, be prepared and learn to play . . . have some fun. Make work a game, too. I do!"

Sally's lessons are clear:

1. Be prepared for anything. Make sure your comforts and needs are provided for first.
2. Don't worry about things. Just pay attention to what is going on around you now. Plan ahead based on what you feel you will need.
3. Share your things with others. Save only what you really need and intend to use and pass on the rest to those who will use it.
4. Simplify your life. Learn to play and make life a game!

Meet Tammy Turtle . . .

Supported by very short legs, Tammy's body is only a few inches from the ground as she travels. In fact, there are times it might appear she is crawling on her belly. With her body so close to the earth, Tammy has a lot of stability and balance.

Many people laugh as Tammy slowly creeps across the sand on her short, stubby legs, carrying her "house" on her back. Can you imagine how it might feel to take your house wherever you go? What might happen if you carried your house with you to school, to play with your friends and so on?

Tammy loves her cozy shell home. No matter where she is she can pull her head, legs and tail inside her "house on legs." The only part of her body that is exposed to anyone or anything that might try to hurt her is a very hard, tough shell that discourages even the most persistent predator, the most fierce storm or the hottest day.

Tammy is very thankful to have a wonderful home in which she can feel safe, warm and protected. She teaches us that any time we feel hurt by what others say or do, or from something we might feel from the outside world, we can go inside our house (inside ourselves) into our own quiet space, to experience our feelings away from other people. When we go inside ourselves it is easier for us to feel God's love. God is inside each of us equally, all the time. When we feel God's love, we feel safe and protected.

Laying her eggs in the warm sand, Tammy knows Mother Earth will protect and nurture her eggs until they hatch. She teaches us to ground our energies, to make the Earth our very best friend. "Make the Earth an important part of your daily life," Tammy says. "Let the Earth take care of you as you take care of the Earth."

Getting back to how slow Tammy moves, we are reminded of the story of the tortoise (turtle) and the hare (rabbit). The rabbit was faster, but hopped around teasing the turtle while the turtle stayed focused on her goal. She moved one step at a time, one foot in front of the other, not letting anything distract her or discourage her. In the end, the turtle won the race.

Tammy's message is:

1. Slow down, move very carefully through each life experience.
2. Think about what you want to accomplish for yourself, then move step by step toward that goal.
3. Obstacles might appear that make you feel you will not reach your goal. However, if you believe in yourself, stay focused on what you want to accomplish, keep moving forward, one step at a time, the obstacles will disappear. You will reach your goal easily and effortlessly. There is nothing we cannot do unless we believe we can't.
4. Whatever you set out to do in life, give it your best. Don't worry about what other people say. Each of us has our own way of doing things. It is best never to compare yourself with another.

Meet Wendy Weasel . . .

Wendy has her eye on one of her favorite foods — chicken. Many henhouses have been visited by Wendy and her friends, making her very unpopular with the farmers in the area.

No matter how hard the farmer tries to protect his chickens, Wendy can find a way into the chicken coop to select a tasty meal. She is *cunning*, meaning she can look at a situation, plan the best approach to achieving her goal and follow through with her plan before anyone can figure out how she got in and out of the challenging situation in such a short time.

Have you ever heard the phrase, "as sly as a weasel," or "he's a weasel?" These are old sayings that describe people who, like Wendy, find ways to outsmart people or situations. You see, Wendy has a lot of energy and can move very fast. She hears what others can't hear and sees what others can't see, or what others choose not to see. These keen senses help her outsmart anyone who might stand in the way of what she calls "progress," that is, having that chicken for dinner.

"Have you ever found yourself in a situation where people were saying one thing to you and you heard it a different way?" Wendy asks. "Perhaps your friends are planning some special event; they are excited. But you don't feel the excitement. You 'feel' there are some problems involved with this event. You can share your feelings with your friends, but if they don't choose to listen, you will need to allow them to learn the lesson in their own way. You, on the other hand, can avoid the event and probably avoid some very uncomfortable situation for yourself."

"We all have gifts," Wendy points out. "But some of us use them and some of us don't. I do. My gifts have really helped me stay out of trouble. I am very grateful to God for giving me the ability to make quick decisions based on what I feel is right for me in the moment. I am grateful I have allowed my intuition to develop. It is a very important tool in my life each day."

Wendy points out:

1. Always trust your own feelings; act on them without hesitation.
2. If you feel confused, stop where you are. Go inside. Ask God to help you make the right decision. Listen carefully and act on what you hear.
3. Help others make the right decision, not by telling them what to do or how to do it, but by teaching them how to listen to their own guidance.

Meet Wesley Wolf . . .

The full Moon shines brightly over Wesley Wolf's mountain home. Wesley and his family are happy to see the Moon and celebrate the occasion by singing (or howling) at the Moon.

Wesley is very loyal to his friends and family. He chooses one mate for life and the pair work together to raise their family, protect each other and share in the food that they find.

Wolves travel in a group called a *pack*. The pack is like a community helping one another. Yet it is very important to Wesley to have private time with his mate and cubs. They find a warm cave to create a home.

"We are all part of God's family," shares Wesley. "But we are also individuals. We each have our own lessons to learn and our own way of learning them. We look different, act different and do things differently from each other. That makes us unique and special.

"God created this beautiful world where we can all experience the gifts of this creation in our own special way. Some people are not happy here. They choose to be unhappy to learn how it feels. I want to be happy. I enjoy my family and community, sharing with others. It makes me feel good. I like the feeling of knowing my "brothers" and "sisters" are looking out for me while I look out for them."

Wesley has developed keen senses of hearing, seeing, smelling, tasting, feeling and knowing. He uses each of his *six* senses very wisely, especially his intuition.

"Your intuition is the most important sense you have available to you in this life. You can do away with all the physical senses and still see, hear, taste, smell and feel, but in a different way. You sense with your intuition."

Remember Wesley's lessons:

1. Celebrate the gifts God has given you . . . the beautiful Earth and all the living things that help you.
2. Be loyal to your friends and family. As you watch out for them, they will watch out for you.
3. Work together in harmony with others but honor your own individuality. Remember that you are very special. No one else has been created exactly like you.
4. Let your intuition be your guide. God speaks to us through our inner voice and God is our greatest source of wisdom and truth.